This Book Belongs to

'Juney Moon' from 'fenske'

written by Richard Kennedy

LITTLE

L · O · V · E

S · O · N · G

illustrated by Petra Mathers

Alfred A. Knopf, Inc. · New York

Library of Congress Cataloging-in-Publication Data
Kennedy, Richard. Little love song / by Richard Kennedy ;
Illustrated by Petra Mathers. p.   cm.   Summary: A
witch's spell enchants a woman and makes her small, and
only the man who loves her can break the spell.
ISBN 0-679-81177-X (trade)
[1. Fairy tales.] I. Mathers, Petra, ill. II. Title.
PZ8.K387Li   1992   [E]—dc20 91-20503

10 9 8 7 6 5 4 3 2 1
Manufactured in the United States.

For Sarah, thanks for the jeebers — R.K.

To Karin — P. M.

My darling's eyes are as bright as tea,
her hair is as orange as fire.
She lives inside a peanut shell,
and I love her or I'm a liar.

She eats raw onions and radish tips,
her dress is a lily bud.
She keeps her cows in a toothpick fence,
and her pigs in a lid of mud.

She bathes each day in a drop of milk,
and dries in a mouse's breath.
A spider web ties up her hair,
and I'll love her until my death.

A cockroach carries her out to shop,
she rides in a cat's ear home.
She sings as sweetly as any lark,
while a grasshopper plays the trombone.

A bumblebee brings her notes to me
in their peapod envelopes.
Sweet words of love on clover leaves,
which I read with a microscope.

She tamed and saddled a dragonfly,
then flew to the porch of my ear.
"My tale is sad but short," she cried.
"If you wish, you may shed a tear.

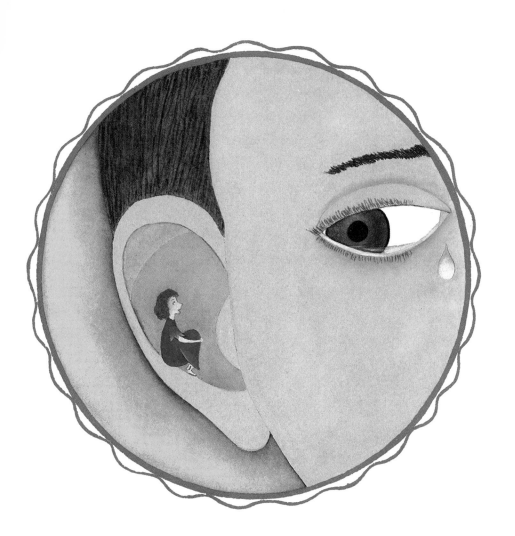

"A witch enchanted me to be small,
for stepping upon her toes.
She had her reasons, I had mine.
Lousy luck, that's the way it goes."

Said I to her, "Oh, my tiny love,
Is there no way to break the spell?
I'd marry you, but think it's hard
to keep house in a peanut shell."

She answered me, "You can break the spell
at night when you're sound asleep.
Just hold and kiss me in a dream,
then I'll be the right size to keep."

And so I lay me down to dream,
after supping on pickles and pie.
I rest my head on a nightingale,
and wiggle my toes at the sky.

My darling's eyes are as bright as tea,
her hair is as orange as fire.
She lives inside a peanut shell,
and I love her or I'm a liar.